DISNEY · PIXAR

INSIDE OUT

FUN BOOK

 JOE BOOKS INC

JOE BOOKS

📚 HarperCollins*PublishersLtd*

Published in the United States by Joe Books
Publisher: Adam Fortier
President: Jody Colero
CEO: Jay Firestone 567 Queen St W, Toronto, ON M5V 2B6
www.joebooks.com

HarperCollins Books may be purchased for educational, business, or sales
promotional use through our Special Markets Department.

HarperCollins Publishers Ltd
2 Bloor Street East, 20th Floor
Toronto, Ontario, Canada
M4W 1A8
www.harpercollins.ca

Library and Archives Canada Cataloguing in Publication information is available upon request.

ISBN 978-1-987955-83-5
First Joe Books and HarperCollins Publishers Ltd Edition: June 2015

1 3 5 7 9 10 8 6 4 2

Printed in USA through Avenue4 Communications at Cenveo/Richmond, Virginia

For information regarding the CPSIA on this printed material, call: (203) 595-3636
and provide reference # RICH - 624189

DESIGNER Mike Paolilli • EDITOR Rob Tokar • SENIOR EDITOR Carolynn Prior •
SENIOR EDITOR Robert Simpson • EXECUTIVE EDITOR Amy Weingartner •
PRODUCTION COORDINATOR Stephanie Alouche

SPECIAL THANKS TO DISNEY PUBLISHING:
Curt Baker • Julie Dorris • Behnoosh Khalili • Manny Mederos • Beatrice Osman

Contents

 Comic: Fear of Night

Comic:
Disgusting Date

 Comic: Joy
for the Win

Comic: VIP Tour

 Fun and Games:
First Memory

DISNEY · PIXAR
INSIDE OUT

the graphic novel

MANUSCRIPT ADAPTATION:
ALESSANDRO FERRARI

LAYOUT:
MASSIMILIANO NARCISO

PENCIL:
**ARIANNA REA, ANDREA GREPPI,
ANDREA SCOPPETTA, FEDERICO MANCUSO**

PAINT:
**ANDREA CAGOL, CRISTINA TONIOLO, ANTONIA EMANUELA ANGRISANI,
SARA SPANO, MASSIMO ROCCA, PATRIZIA ZANGRILLI**

ARTIST COORDINATION:
TOMATOFARM

EDITORIAL PAGES:
CO-D S.R.L. – MILANO

PRE-PRESS:
EDIZIONI BD S.R.L.

SPECIAL THANKS TO
**CAITLIN KENNEDY, VALERIE LAPOINTE, SCOTT TILLEY,
LAURA UYEDA, SAMANTHA WILSON**

cinestory comic

ADAPTED BY
JOELLE SELLNER

SENIOR EDITORS
**CAROLYNN PRIOR
ROBERT SIMPSON**

EXECUTIVE EDITOR
AMY WEINGARTNER

PRODUCTION COORDINATOR
STEPHANIE ALOUCHE

LETTERING AND LAYOUT
**SALVADOR NAVARRO, ESTER SALGUERO,
EDUARDO ALPUENTE, ALBERTO GARRIDO,
PUSTE, AND ERNESTO LOVERA**

DESIGNER
HEIDI ROUX

SPECIAL THANKS
**RACHEL ALOR, CURT BAKER, KELLY BONBRIGHT, DEBORAH CICHOCKI
JULIE DORRIS, MOLLY JONES, BEHNOOSH KHALILI, CYNTHIA LUSK
VICTORIA R. MANLEY, MANNY MEDEROS, BEATRICE OSMAN, NIK SIEFKE
SCOTT TILLEY, SHIHO TILLEY**

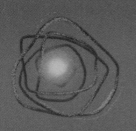

"All right everyone, fresh start!
We are gonna have a good day, which will
turn into a good week, which will turn into
a good year, which turns into a good LIFE!"

joy

INSIDE OUT FUN BOOK

riley's emotions

The Five Emotions live and work in Headquarters, which is located in the center of Riley's mind.

sadness

Always been the **"glass half empty" type**, Sadness would really love to be more optimistic. But she often has no choice but to collapse into a puddle of sorrow when faced with everyday miseries!

fear

It's so hard to cope with **all the terrifying stuff** in the world: that strange noise coming from the basement at night, roller skates, puppies... For Fear, 99% of things are dangerous and/or possibly fatal.

joy

anger

disgust

Always looking at the bright side of life, Joy has been Riley's lead Emotion since day one. With **her unstoppable optimism** and can-do attitude, Joy does her best to keep Riley positive no matter what happens.

Anger tries to keep his cool, but it's difficult when there's so much unfairness in the world. He's always there to fight the good fight against injustices such as lack of cookies, naps, and broccoli on pizza.

Disgust has always been proud of her **refined tastes**. Her job is to keep Riley from being poisoned, physically or socially, and to do this she carefully detects and avoids all the disgusting things in life.

dad

Dad has always been a caring and involved father to his only daughter, Riley. **A good guy** and a devoted husband, now Dad is finally able to fulfill a lifelong dream of his own startup company in San Francisco.

mom

With her boundless enthusiasm, Mom keeps the family stable and in check. She's a **tireless and cheerful** mother, and an unwavering supporter of Dad's new business venture.

riley

Riley is a cheerful 11-year-old girl, with a **spirited imagination**, a happy-go-lucky personality, and a real passion for hockey! But when her family moves from Minnesota to San Francisco, adjusting to a new city shakes her confidence...

the story of the movie in comics

INSIDE OUT FUN BOOK

I'M SADNESS.

OH, HELLO. I'M JOY.

AND THAT WAS JUST THE BEGINNING.

THAT'S FEAR.

AHH! LOOK OUT! NO!

HE'S REALLY GOOD AT KEEPING RILEY SAFE

THIS IS DISGUST.

THAT IS NOT BRIGHTLY COLORED OR SHAPED LIKE A DINOSAUR. HOLD ON... IT'S BROCCOLI!

SHE KEEPS RILEY FROM BEING POISONED. PHYSICALLY AND SOCIALLY.

AND THAT'S ANGER.

WAIT. DID DAD JUST SAY WE COULDN'T HAVE DESSERT?

HE CARES VERY DEEPLY ABOUT THINGS BEING FAIR

OH, AN AIRPLANE. WE GOT AN AIRPLANE, EVERYBODY!

AND YOU'VE MET SADNESS. SHE, WELL... I'M NOT SURE WHAT SHE DOES. SHE'S GOOD, WE'RE GOOD. IT'S ALL GREAT!

ANYWAY, THESE ARE RILEY'S MEMORIES ...

INSIDE OUT FUN BOOK

... AND THEY'RE MOSTLY HAPPY, YOU'LL NOTICE, NOT TO BRAG.

BUT THE *REALLY* IMPORTANT ONES ARE OVER HERE. I DON'T WANT TO GET TOO TECHNICAL, BUT THESE ARE CALLED *CORE MEMORIES.*

EACH ONE CAME FROM A SUPER IMPORTANT TIME IN RILEY'S LIFE. LIKE WHEN SHE FIRST SCORED A GOAL. THAT WAS SO AMAZING...

AND EACH CORE MEMORY POWERS A DIFFERENT ASPECT OF RILEY'S PERSONALITY...

RRRRR

FZZZ

INSIDE OUT FUN BOOK

INSIDE OUT FUN BOOK

GOODNIGHT, KIDDO.

GOODNIGHT, DAD.

AND... WE'RE OUT! ANOTHER PERFECT DAY!

LET'S GET THOSE MEMORIES DOWN TO LONG TERM.

CLACK

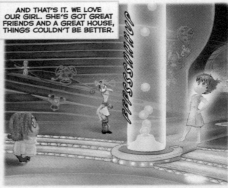

AND THAT'S IT. WE LOVE OUR GIRL. SHE'S GOT GREAT FRIENDS AND A GREAT HOUSE, THINGS COULDN'T BE BETTER.

FFFSSSHHHP

AFTER ALL, RILEY'S ELEVEN NOW. WHAT COULD HAPPEN?

BUT ONE DAY...

WHA...

AIIIIGHH!!!

A MOVING VAN TAKES ALL OF RILEY'S BELONGINGS AWAY AND SHE TRAVELS ACROSS THE COUNTRY WITH HER PARENTS, FROM MINNESOTA...

... TO SAN FRANCISCO, CALIFORNIA!

HEY, LOOK! THE GOLDEN GATE BRIDGE! ISN'T THAT GREAT?!

WE'RE ALMOST TO OUR NEW HOUSE, RILEY!

BUT THE NEW HOME IS NOT SO GREAT...

WE'RE SUPPOSED TO LIVE HERE?

DO WE HAVE TO?

I'M TELLING YOU, IT SMELLS LIKE SOMETHING DIED IN HERE.

CAN YOU DIE FROM MOVING?

INSIDE OUT FUN BOOK

INSIDE OUT FUN BOOK

INSIDE OUT FUN BOOK

INSIDE OUT FUN BOOK

INSIDE OUT FUN BOOK

INSIDE OUT FUN BOOK

INSIDE OUT FUN BOOK

INSIDE OUT FUN BOOK

...OY COLLECTS ALL THE ...ORE MEMORIES, BUT...

NO! NO! NO!

FFFSSSHHHHHVVVP

NO!

FFFSSSHHH

NOOOO!

FFFSSSHHHHVVVP

CAN I SAY THAT CURSE WORD NOW?

THANK YOU, RILEY. I KNOW IT CAN BE TOUGH MOVING TO A NEW PLACE, BUT WE'RE HAPPY TO HAVE YOU HERE.

JOY AND SADNESS ROCKET DOWN THE TUBE...

AHHHH

AHHHH

... AND LAND IN LONG TERM MEMORY!

RILEY'S ISLANDS OF PERSONALITY... THEY'RE ALL DOWN! THIS IS BAD...

NO, LOOK... WE CAN FIX THIS. WE JUST HAVE TO GET BACK TO HEADQUARTERS, PLUG THE CORE MEMORIES IN, AND RILEY WILL BE BACK TO NORMAL.

RILEY HAS NO CORE MEMORIES, NO PERSONALITY ISLANDS AND NO...

WHAT... WHAT IS IT?

YOU! YOU'RE NOT IN HEADQUARTERS! WITHOUT YOU, RILEY CAN'T BE HAPPY.

WE GOTTA GET YOU BACK UP THERE...

INSIDE OUT FUN BOOK

LATER THAT EVENING, RILEY IS HAVING DINNER WITH MOM AND DAD...

I FOUND A JUNIOR HOCKEY LEAGUE RIGHT HERE IN SAN FRANCISCO. AND GET THIS... TRYOUTS ARE TOMORROW AFTER SCHOOL. WHAT LUCK, RIGHT?

HOCKEY?

UH-OH. WHAT DO WE DO?

YOU PRETEND TO BE JOY!

WON'T IT BE GREAT TO BE BACK OUT ON THE ICE?

OH YEAH, THAT SOUNDS *FANTASTIC.*

WHAT WAS THAT? THAT WASN'T ANYTHING LIKE JOY.

UH, BECAUSE I'M *NOT* JOY.

THE SITUATION GETS WORSE WHEN ANGER TAKES CONTROL...

RILEY, IS EVERYTHING OKAY?

RILEY, I DO *NOT* LIKE THIS NEW ATTITUDE.

OH, I'LL SHOW YOU ATTITUDE, OLD MAN!

WHAT IS YOUR PROBLEM? JUST LEAVE ME ALONE!

THAT IS IT! GO TO YOUR ROOM! NOW!

INSIDE OUT FUN BOOK

INSIDE OUT FUN BOOK

INSIDE OUT FUN BOOK

INSIDE OUT FUN BOOK

INSIDE RILEY'S MIND...

RRRRRRRUMBLE

OH NO...

... FRIENDSHIP ISLAND FALLS AWAY...

RRRRRUMBLE

... AND JOY SEES THE FRIENDSHIP CORE MEMORY FADE IN HER ARMS...

!

GOOD-BYE, FRIENDSHIP. HELLO, LONELINESS.

WE'LL JUST HAVE TO GO THE LONG WAY...

CLONK

?

HEY! WAIT! STOP!

INSIDE OUT FUN BOOK

RILEY LOVED PLAYING WITH YOU! REMEMBER YOUR ROCKET?

OF COURSE! IT RUNS ON SONG POWER.

WAIT. I KNOW YOU... YOU'RE BING BONG! RILEY'S IMAGINARY FRIEND!

YOU *DO* KNOW ME!

SO WHAT ARE YOU DOING OUT HERE?

WELL, THERE'S NOT MUCH CALL FOR IMAGINARY FRIENDS LATELY... SO, UH, YOU KNOW... I'M...

HEY, DON'T BE SAD. WHEN I GET BACK UP TO HEADQUARTERS, I'LL MAKE SURE RILEY REMEMBERS YOU.

YOU WILL?!?

THIS IS THE GREATEST DAY OF MY LIFE! DOOOOOH!

!

WHAT'S GOING ON?

I CRY CANDY. TRY THE CARAMEL, IT'S DELICIOUS.

INSIDE OUT FUN BOOK

41

INSIDE OUT FUN BOOK

INSIDE OUT FUN BOOK

43

INSIDE OUT FUN BOOK

INSIDE RILEY'S MIND, ANOTHER ISLAND CRUMBLES...

OH NO... NO, SHE LOVES HOCKEY...

RRRRUMBLE

BING BONG, WE HAVE TO GET TO THAT STATION.

SURE THING. THIS WAY, JUST PAST THE...

:GASP!: MY ROCKET! WAIT!

RILEY AND I, WE'RE STILL USING THAT ROCKET! IT STILL HAS SOME SONG POWER LEFT!

INSIDE OUT FUN BOOK

THAT SOUNDS AMAZING. I BET RILEY LIKED IT.

OH, SHE DID... WE WERE BEST FRIENDS...

YEAH. IT'S SAD.

I'M OKAY NOW.

C'MON, THE TRAIN STATION IS THIS WAY!

?!

HOW DID YOU DO THAT?

OH, I DON'T KNOW. HE WAS SAD SO I LISTENED TO WHAT--

AND FINALLY, JOY, SADNESS AND BING BONG REACH THE TRAIN OF THOUGHT!

WE MADE IT! WE'RE FINALLY GOING TO GET HOME!

INSIDE OUT FUN BOOK

47

BACK IN HER BEDROOM, RILEY IS STILL AWAKE...

ON A SCALE OF ONE TO TEN, I GIVE THIS DAY AN F.

WHY DON'T WE QUIT STANDING AROUND AND DO SOMETHING.

LIKE WHAT, GENIUS?

LIKE THIS!

WHAT IS IT?

OH, NOTHING... JUST THE BEST IDEA EVER.

WHAT?

ALL THE GOOD CORE MEMORIES WERE MADE IN MINNESOTA. ERGO, WE GO BACK TO MINNESOTA AND MAKE MORE!

YOU CAN'T BE SERIOUS.

HEY. OUR LIFE WAS PERFECT UNTIL MOM AND DAD DECIDED TO MOVE TO SAN FRAN STINKTOWN.

WAIT, HOLD ON... SHOULDN'T WE JUST SLEEP ON THIS OR SOMETHING?

FINE. LET'S SLEEP ON IT.

BECAUSE I'M SURE JOLLY FUN-FILLED TIMES ARE JUST AROUND THE CORNER...

THE TRAIN OF THOUGHT STOPS. IT DOESN'T RUN WHILE RILEY IS ASLEEP...

WE'RE STUCK HERE UNTIL MORNING?

WE CAN'T WAIT THAT LONG!

HOW ABOUT WE WAKE HER UP?

SHORTLY AFTER, AT DREAM PRODUCTIONS...

OKAY, HOW ARE WE GONNA WAKE HER UP?

WELL, SHE WAKES UP SOMETIMES WHEN SHE HAS A SCARY DREAM. WE COULD SCARE HER.

SCARE HER? NO, NO, SHE'S BEEN THROUGH ENOUGH ALREADY.

WE'RE GONNA MAKE RILEY SO HAPPY THAT SHE'LL WAKE UP WITH EXHILARATION! PUT THIS ON...

DON'T LET ANYTHING HAPPEN TO THESE.

GOT IT!

INSIDE OUT FUN BOOK

REMEMBER, PLAY TO THE CAMERA, EVERYONE! RILEY IS THE CAMERA!

WE ARE ON IN 5, 4, 3...

AT HEADQUARTERS, FEAR IS ON DREAM DUTY...

EW, LOOK! HER TEETH ARE FALLING OUT!

TEETH FALLING OUT... I'M USED TO THAT ONE.

SUDDENLY...

BARK! BARK! BARK!

WHAT IS GOING ON?

SADNESS, WHAT ARE YOU DOING?! COME BACK HERE!

R!!!!!P

IT'S JUST A DREAM! IT'S JUST A DREAM!

SADNESS! YOU ARE RUINING THIS DREAM! YOU'RE SCARING HER!

BUT LOOK...

ASLEEP

ASLEEP AWAKE

... IT'S WORKING!

INSIDE OUT FUN BOOK

THE TRAIN'S NOT RUNNING. WE STILL HAVE TO WAKE UP RILEY.

JOY REALIZES SADNESS WAS RIGHT ABOUT SCARING RILEY AWAKE...

... SO SHE LEADS JANGLES TO DREAM PRODUCTIONS!

WHO'S THE BIRTHDAY GIRL?

CRASH

BLAM

BOOM

AHHHHH!

AIIIII!

!!!

AND SO...

WE MADE IT! GUESS WHO'S ON THEIR WAY TO HEADQUARTERS?

WE ARE!

INSIDE OUT FUN BOOK

53

MEANWHILE, AT HEADQUARTERS...

TIME TO TAKE ACTION.

CLICK

SHE TOOK IT. THERE'S NO TURNING BACK.

HOW'RE WE GONNA GET TO MINNESOTA FROM HERE?

WE'RE TAKING THE BUS. THERE'S ONE LEAVING TOMORROW.

A TICKET COSTS MONEY. HOW DO WE GET MONEY?

MOM'S PURSE.

GASP! YOU WOULDN'T!

MOM AND DAD GOT US INTO THIS MESS. THEY CAN PAY TO GET US OUT.

AS SOON AS RILEY TAKES THE CREDIT CARD...

INSIDE OUT FUN BOOK

INSIDE OUT FUN BOOK

THE NEXT MORNING RILEY PRETENDS SHE'S GOING TO SCHOOL...

HAVE A GREAT DAY, SWEETHEART.

JOY! IT'S TOO DANGEROUS! WE WON'T MAKE IT IN TIME!

BUT THAT'S OUR ONLY WAY BACK!

A BIG SHELF COLLAPSES AND A RECALL TUBE IS EXPOSED...

A RECALL TUBE!

WE CAN GET RECALLED!

WHOA! SADNESS!

STOP! YOU'RE HURTING RILEY!

OH NO! I DID IT AGAIN!

IF YOU GET IN HERE, THESE CORE MEMORIES WILL GET SAD.

JOY?

I'M SORRY! RILEY NEEDS TO BE HAPPY.

WOOOOH

THE RUMBLING BREAKS
THE TUBE APART...

RRRRRRUMBLE

... AND THE CLIFFSIDE
CRUMBLES AWAY.

JOY!

STUCK IN THE MEMORY DUMP, JOY AND BING BONG ARE DESTINED TO BE FORGOTTEN...

I JUST WANTED RILEY TO BE HAPPY. AND NOW...

?

THE MEMORY TURNS BLUE AND JOY REMEMBERS WHAT SADNESS SAID ABOUT THAT DAY...

"IT WAS THE DAY THE PRAIRIE DOGS LOST THE BIG PLAYOFF GAME. RILEY MISSED THE WINNING SHOT. SHE FELT AWFUL. SHE WANTED TO QUIT."

WE HAVE TO GET BACK UP THERE!

JOY, WE'RE STUCK DOWN HERE. WE MIGHT AS WELL BE ON ANOTHER PLANET.

MOM AND DAD... THE TEAM... THEY CAME TO HELP BECAUSE OF SADNESS!

ANOTHER PLANET!

♪ WHO'S YOUR FRIEND WHO LIKES TO PLAY? BING BONG, BING BONG! ♪

!

INSIDE OUT FUN BOOK

INSIDE OUT FUN BOOK

INSIDE RILEY'S HEAD. SADNESS IS FLOATING AWAY...

SADNESS! WAIT!

JUST LET ME GO! RILEY'S BETTER OFF WITHOUT ME. I ONLY MAKE EVERYTHING WORSE.

BUT JOY KNOWS WHAT TO DO...

DID YOU MEAN WHAT YOU SAID BEFORE?

I WOULD DIE FOR RILEY!

TIME TO PROVE IT!

USING THE IMAGINARY BOYFRIENDS AS A TOWER, JOY FALLS ONTO FAMILY ISLAND...

... BOUNCES OFF A TRAMPOLINE THERE...

BOING

... GRABS ONTO SADNESS...

GOTCHA!

... AND THEY BOTH GO BACK TOWARD HEADQUARTERS!

INSIDE OUT FUN BOOK

INSIDE OUT FUN BOOK

I KNOW YOU DON'T WANT ME TO, BUT... I MISS HOME. I MISS MINNESOTA.

YOU NEED ME TO BE HAPPY, BUT... I WANT MY OLD FRIENDS, AND MY HOCKEY TEAM... I WANNA GO HOME. PLEASE DON'T BE MAD.

OH, SWEETIE.

WE'RE NOT MAD. YOU KNOW WHAT? I MISS MINNESOTA TOO. I MISS THE WOODS WHERE WE TOOK HIKES.

AND THE BACKYARD WHERE YOU USED TO PLAY.

SPRING LAKE, WHERE YOU LEARNED TO SKATE.

...AT HEADQUARTERS, A NEW CORE MEMORY IS CREATED...

WHIRR

...AND JOY AND SADNESS FINALLY BECOME A TEAM.

INSIDE OUT FUN BOOK

Inside Out
Comics

Script: Alessandro Ferrari & Behnoosh Khalili   Layouts: Antonello Dalena   Cleanups: Andrea Greppi
Paints: Cristina Toniolo & Sara Spano   Letters: Chris Dickey   © 2015 Disney/Pixar

INSIDE OUT FUN BOOK

INSIDE OUT FUN BOOK

Script: Alessandro Ferrari & Behnoosh Khalili Layouts: Antonello Dalena Cleanups: Andrea Greppi Paints: Livio Cacciatore Letters: Chris Dickey

INSIDE OUT FUN BOOK

INSIDE OUT FUN BOOK

INSIDE OUT FUN BOOK

Script: Alessandro Ferrari & Behnoosh Khalili Layouts: Antonello Daiena Cleanups: Andrea Greppi

FINALLY, IT'S NEW YEAR'S EVE. RILEY'S 8 YEARS OLD...AND WE GET TO STAY UP UNTIL MIDNIGHT FOR THE FIRST TIME!

FANTASTIC! THIS IS SO FESTIVE!

SO YOU'RE SURE THE WORLD WON'T BE ENDING AT MIDNIGHT, RIGHT?!

WE BETTER GET THE SAME AMOUNT OF SNACKS AS MOM AND DAD!

HEY, RILEY, I WANT YOU TO MEET A NEW FRIEND. THIS IS TOM. YOU'LL BOTH BE SITTING AT THIS SPECIAL TABLE.

HI, I'M TOM. WANNA PULL MY FINGER?

IS THIS GUY FOR REAL?

HOW DARE THEY PUT HIM AT THIS TABLE!

YEAH, HOW OLD IS HE? 7?

HE SHOULD BE AT THE *BABY* TABLE.

HERE'S A FLOWER FOR YOU, MY SWEET.

THERE IS NOTHING SWEET ABOUT THIS SITUATION!

BROCCOLI!!! GROSS! THAT'S NOT A FLOWER!

WHAT IS HE TRYING TO DO, KILL US?

I'M DIGGING FOR A TREASURE FOR YOU.

UGH, THIS GUY *IS* GROSS.

I'LL HANDLE THIS.

INSIDE OUT FUN BOOK

INSIDE OUT FUN BOOK

Script: Alessandro Ferrari & Behnoosh Khalili   Layouts: Antonello Dalena
Cleanups: Andrea Greppi   Paints: Antonia Angrisani   Letters: Chris Dickey
© 2015 Disney/Pixar

INSIDE OUT FUN BOOK

INSIDE OUT FUN BOOK

INSIDE OUT FUN BOOK

SPARKLE PONY MOUNTAIN

GET YOUR NOSE OUT OF THAT MAP. THIS ONE YOU'VE GOT TO SEE TO BELIEVE!

WE'LL SEE ABOUT THAT.

THEY'RE REAL?! I'VE ONLY HEARD RUMORS.

OH, THEY'RE REAL, ALL RIGHT. AND THEY CAN BE QUITE WILD.

BUT WE SHOULD STILL RIDE THEM.

YEEHAW! FUN FACT: SPARKLE PONIES LOVE DOUGHNUTS.

WHY DO I HAVE TO GET THE ONE ANNOYED PONY?

HE'S ONLY ANNOYED BECAUSE YOU ARE. YOUR SMILES GIVE THEM SPARKLE POWER. GO AHEAD, TRY A SMILE.

SEE, I TOLD YA IT'D WORK.

INSIDE OUT FUN BOOK

INSIDE OUT FUN BOOK

INSIDE OUT FUN BOOK

Inside Out
Activities

first memory

Help Joy save Riley's
first happy memory
by crossing out all the pairs
of spheres with an identical
image inside. The one
left over is Riley's
first memory.

DIFFICULTY: TOUGH

INSIDE OUT FUN BOOK

half empty glass

Sadness is a **glass-half-empty** kind of Emotion, that's why she's always **blue**! Color the glasses according to the number of **blue drops** falling in them to find out which glass is half empty.

DIFFICULTY: TOUGHER

A B C D E F G H

RAIN MAKES EVERYTHING FEEL DROOPY.

headquarters in a whirl

DIFFERENT EMOTIONS

The Emotions deal with different things every day, as Riley does. Find the 10 little differences between the two pictures below.

DIFFICULTY: TOUGHER

INSIDE OUT FUN BOOK

EMOTIONAL CROSSWORDS

DIFFICULTY: TOUGH!

See how the Emotions and memories all fit together by filling in the **crossword** puzzle.

Crossword answers:
- m e m o r i e s
- J o y
- D i s g u s t
- s a d n e s s
- a n g e r
- f e a r

SCRAMBLED CONSOLE

DIFFICULTY: TOUGHEST!

As Riley grows up, the console in Headquarters becomes much larger and more complex. Find the correct position for each part of the console and write in the number.

1 2 3 4 5 6 7 8 9 10

5 10 8 7 1 9 4 3 6 2

anger game

Don't let Anger **lose control**, that could get Riley into trouble. **Count** the flames in the four paths leading to the console, and write each number to find the safest one with the **fewest flames**!

start

A
B
C
D

finish

INSIDE OUT FUN BOOK

When Joy, Sadness and Bing Bong enter Abstract Thought, they break down into strange shapes. Can you complete the picture at the bottom of this page with the pieces below?

DIFFICULTY: TOUGH

mind maze

Joy, Sadness, and Bing Bong are trying to get to Headquarters. Solve the maze through Long Term Memory to see where it leads them on their journey.

DIFFICULTY: TOUGHER

INSIDE OUT FUN BOOK

DREAM PRODUCTIONS

THE SUBCONSCIOUS

IMAGINATION LAND

ABSTRACT THOUGHT

INSIDE OUT FUN BOOK

sweet sadness

When Riley's old imaginary friend Bing Bong is sad, he cries candy! Keep him from crying by choosing the candy stream with the lowest weeping power! On a piece of paper, calculate it using the legend on the right.

DIFFICULTY: TOUGHER

CANDY WEEPING POWER

1	3	5	7	9	10

INSIDE OUT FUN BOOK

how are you feeling?

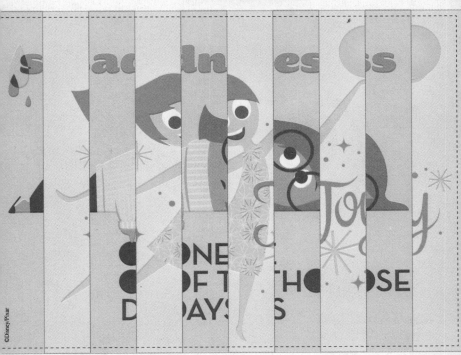

INSTRUCTIONS

1 Cut out the mini poster along the dotted lines.

2 Fold the mini poster along the fold lines, like a fan.

3 Choose your feeling... happy or sad?

  JOYFUL

 SAD

Scenes from the Inside Out Cinestory Comic

INSIDE OUT

HEY, LOOK! THE GOLDEN GATE BRIDGE! ISN'T THAT GREAT?

IT'S NOT MADE OUT OF SOLID GOLD LIKE WE THOUGHT, WHICH IS KIND OF A DISAPPOINTMENT, BUT STILL!

I SURE AM GLAD YOU TOLD ME EARTHQUAKES ARE A MYTH, JOY. OTHERWISE I'D BE TERRIFIED RIGHT NOW.

UH... YEAH...

FUTURE IS SHAKY!

96   **INSIDE OUT FUN BOOK**

WHY DON'T WE JUST LIVE IN THIS SMELLY CAR? WE'VE ALREADY BEEN IN IT FOREVER.

WHICH ACTUALLY WAS REALLY LUCKY, BECAUSE THAT GAVE US PLENTY OF TIME TO THINK ABOUT WHAT OUR NEW HOUSE IS GOING TO LOOK LIKE!

WHAT?! LET'S REVIEW THE TOP FIVE DAYDREAMS.

OOH! THAT LOOKS SAFE.

OH, NICE.

OOH, THIS WILL BE GREAT FOR RILEY! OH, NO, NO, NO...

THIS ONE.

UGH, JOY. FOR THE LAST TIME, SHE CAN'T LIVE IN A COOKIE.

INSIDE OUT FUN BOOK

THAT'S THE ONE! IT COMES WITH A DRAGON.

NOW WE'RE GETTING CLOSE, I CAN FEEL IT. HERE IT IS, HERE'S OUR NEW HOUSE... AND...

MAYBE IT'S NICE ON THE INSIDE!

INSIDE OUT FUN BOOK

INSIDE OUT FUN BOOK

INSIDE OUT FUN BOOK

INSIDE OUT FUN BOOK

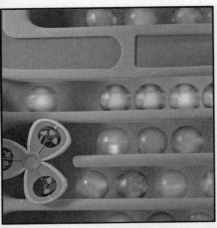

INSIDE OUT FUN BOOK 103

INSIDE OUT FUN BOOK

ALRIGHT. GOOD-BYE.

WELL, GUESS WHAT? THE MOVING VAN WON'T BE HERE UNTIL THURSDAY.

YOU'RE KIDDING!

THE VAN IS LOST?! THIS IS THE WORST DAY EVER.

YOU SAID IT WOULD BE HERE YESTERDAY!

I KNOW THAT'S WHAT I SAID. THAT'S WHAT THEY TOLD ME!

MOM AND DAD ARE STRESSED OUT!

THEY'RE ARGUING! WHAT ARE WE GOING TO DO?

THIS IS SO STRESSFUL.

WHAT IS THEIR PROBLEM?

INSIDE OUT FUN BOOK

INSIDE OUT FUN BOOK

INSIDE OUT FUN BOOK

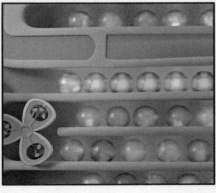

UGH. SORRY, HOLD ON, HOLD ON.

RIIIIING!

HELLO?

WAIT. WHA -- ?

YOU'RE KIDDING. ALRIGHT. STALL FOR ME. I'LL BE RIGHT THERE.

THE INVESTOR'S SUPPOSED TO SHOW UP ON THURSDAY, NOT TODAY. I GOTTA GO.

IT'S OKAY. WE GET IT.

INSIDE OUT FUN BOOK

YOU'RE THE BEST. THANKS, HON.

SEE YOU, SWEETIE.

DAD JUST LEFT US.

OH, HE DOESN'T LOVE US ANYMORE. THAT'S SAD.

I SHOULD DRIVE, RIGHT?

JOY? WHAT ARE YOU DOING?

UH, JUST UH, GIMMIE ONE SECOND...

YOU KNOW WHAT I'VE REALIZED? RILEY HASN'T HAD LUNCH!

REMEMBER?

PIZZA

INSIDE OUT FUN BOOK

INSIDE OUT FUN BOOK

WHAT THE HECK IS THAT?!

WHO PUTS BROCCOLI ON PIZZA?

THAT'S IT. I'M DONE.

CONGRATULATIONS, SAN FRANCISCO, YOU'VE RUINED PIZZA! FIRST THE HAWAIIANS AND NOW YOU!

WHAT KIND OF A PIZZA PLACE ONLY SERVES ONE KIND OF PIZZA?

MUST BE A SAN FRANCISCO THING, HUH? STILL, IT'S NOT AS BAD AS THE SOUP AT THAT DINER IN NEBRASKA.

OH YEAH. THE SPOON STOOD UP IN THE SOUP BY ITSELF! THAT WAS DISGUSTING.

OH GOOD. FAMILY IS RUNNING.

INSIDE OUT FUN BOOK

INSIDE OUT FUN BOOK

INSIDE OUT FUN BOOK

INSIDE OUT FUN BOOK

GOOD GOING, SADNESS. NOW WHEN RILEY THINKS OF THAT MOMENT WITH DAD, SHE'S GONNA FEEL SAD. BRAVO.

I'M SORRY, JOY... I DON'T REALLY KNOW -- I THOUGHT MAYBE IF YOU -- IF YOU -- IF..I MEAN...

JOY, WE'VE GOT A STAIRWAY COMING UP.

JUST DON'T TOUCH ANY OTHER MEMORIES UNTIL WE FIGURE OUT WHAT'S GOING ON.

OKAY.

INSIDE OUT FUN BOOK

INSIDE OUT FUN BOOK

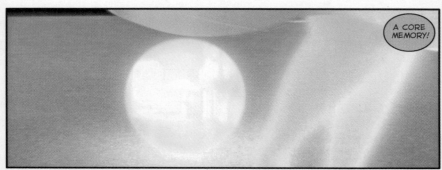

INSIDE OUT FUN BOOK

INSIDE OUT FUN BOOK 119

INSIDE OUT FUN BOOK

INSIDE OUT FUN BOOK

INSIDE OUT FUN BOOK

INSIDE OUT FUN BOOK

STILL NO MOVING VAN. NOW THEY'RE SAYING IT WON'T BE HERE 'TIL TUESDAY, CAN YOU BELIEVE IT?

TOOT TOOT TOOT!

WHERE'S DAD?

ON THE PHONE. THIS NEW VENTURE'S KEEPING HIM PRETTY BUSY.

I REST MY CASE!

YOUR DAD'S A LITTLE STRESSED -- YOU KNOW, ABOUT GETTING HIS NEW COMPANY UP AND RUNNING...

NOW FOR A FEW WELL-PLACED WITHERING SCOWLS.

I GUESS ALL I REALLY WANT TO SAY IS, THANK YOU.

HUH?

INSIDE OUT FUN BOOK

YOU KNOW, THROUGH ALL THIS CONFUSION YOU'VE STAYED...WELL, YOU'VE STAYED OUR HAPPY GIRL. YOUR DAD'S BEEN UNDER A LOT OF PRESSURE...

...BUT IF YOU AND I CAN KEEP SMILING, IT WOULD BE A BIG HELP. WE CAN DO THAT FOR HIM, RIGHT?

WHOA. WELL.

YEAH! SURE.

WHAT DID WE DO TO DESERVE YOU?

INSIDE OUT FUN BOOK 125

SWEET DREAMS.

GOOD NIGHT.

WELL, YOU CAN'T ARGUE WITH MOM. "HAPPY" IT IS.

TEAM HAPPY! SOUNDS GREAT!

I'M, TOTALLY BEHIND YOU, JOY.

LOOKS LIKE WE'RE GOING INTO REM. I GOT DREAM DUTY, SO I'LL TAKE CARE OF SENDING THESE TO LONG TERM.

GREAT DAY TODAY, GUYS! SLEEP WELL, TEAM HAPPY!

INSIDE OUT FUN BOOK

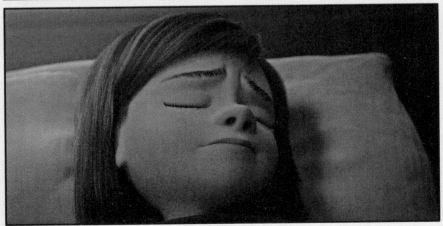

INSIDE OUT FUN BOOK 127

INSIDE OUT FUN BOOK

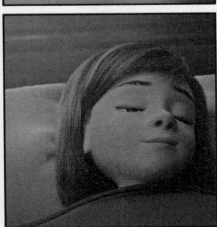

INSIDE OUT FUN BOOK

129

INSIDE OUT FUN BOOK

JOY. YES, JOY? YOU'LL BE IN CHARGE OF THE CONSOLE, KEEPING RILEY HAPPY ALL DAY LONG. AND MAY I ADD, I LOVE YOUR DRESS, IT'S ADORABLE.

OH, THIS OL' THING? THANK YOU SO MUCH. I LOVE THE WAY IT TWIRLS...

TOOT TOOT

TRAIN OF THOUGHT! RIGHT ON SCHEDULE.

ANGER. UNLOAD THE DAYDREAMS. I ORDERED EXTRA IN CASE THINGS GOT SLOW IN CLASS.

MIGHT COME IN HANDY, IF THIS NEW SCHOOL IS FULL OF BORING USELESS CLASSES, WHICH IT PROBABLY WILL BE...

INSIDE OUT FUN BOOK

INSIDE OUT FUN BOOK

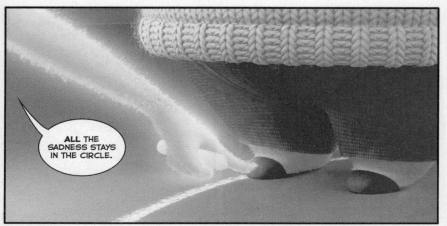

ALL THE SADNESS STAYS IN THE CIRCLE.

SEE? YOU'RE A PRO AT THIS! ISN'T THIS FUN?!

NO.

ATTA GIRL.

ALRIGHT, EVERYONE, FRESH START! WE ARE GONNA HAVE A GOOD DAY, WHICH WILL TURN INTO A GOOD WEEK, WHICH WILL TURN INTO A GOOD YEAR...

...WHICH TURNS INTO A GOOD LIFE!

INSIDE OUT FUN BOOK

INSIDE OUT FUN BOOK

INSIDE OUT FUN BOOK

INSIDE OUT FUN BOOK

INSIDE OUT FUN BOOK

INSIDE OUT FUN BOOK

INSIDE OUT FUN BOOK

YEAH, IT GETS PRETTY COLD. THE LAKES FREEZE OVER AND THAT'S WHEN WE PLAY HOCKEY.

I'M ON A GREAT TEAM. WE'RE CALLED THE PRAIRIE DOGS. MY FRIEND MEG PLAYS FORWARD.

AND MY DAD'S THE COACH. PRETTY MUCH EVERYONE IN MY FAMILY SKATES.

IT'S A KIND OF FAMILY TRADITION. WE GO OUT ON THE LAKE ALMOST EVERY WEEKEND.

Read on for another scene!

SO AS IT TURNS OUT, THE GREEN TRASH CAN IS NOT RECYCLING, IT'S FOR GREENS.

LIKE COMPOST. AND EGGSHELLS.

MMM.

AND THE BLUE ONE IS RECYCLING. AND THE BLACK ONE IS TRASH.

RILEY IS ACTING SO WEIRD. WHY IS SHE ACTING SO WEIRD?

WHAT DO YOU EXPECT? ALL THE ISLANDS ARE DOWN.

INSIDE OUT FUN BOOK

JOY WOULD KNOW WHAT TO DO.

THAT'S IT! UNTIL SHE GETS BACK, WE JUST DO WHAT JOY WOULD DO.

GREAT IDEA! ANGER, FEAR, DISGUST. HOW ARE WE SUPPOSED TO BE HAPPY?

HEY, RILEY. I'VE GOT SOME GOOD NEWS!

I FOUND A JUNIOR HOCKEY LEAGUE RIGHT HERE IN SAN FRANCISCO.

AND GET THIS: TRYOUTS ARE TOMORROW AFTER SCHOOL. WHAT LUCK, RIGHT?

HOCKEY?

INSIDE OUT FUN BOOK

INSIDE OUT FUN BOOK

INSIDE OUT FUN BOOK

INSIDE OUT FUN BOOK

INSIDE OUT FUN BOOK

INSIDE OUT FUN BOOK 149

INSIDE OUT FUN BOOK

INSIDE OUT FUN BOOK

INSIDE OUT FUN BOOK

INSIDE OUT FUN BOOK 153

INSIDE OUT FUN BOOK

INSIDE OUT FUN BOOK

WAAH-WAAH-WAAH!

YOU HEARD THAT, GENTLEMEN. DEFCON 2.

LISTEN, YOUNG LADY, I DON'T KNOW WHERE THIS DISRESPECTFUL ATTITUDE CAME FROM --

YOU WANT A PIECE OF THIS, POPS? COME AND GET IT!

HERE IT COMES... PREPARE THE FOOT.

INSIDE OUT FUN BOOK

WE'RE GONNA WALK OUT THERE? ON THAT?

IT'S THE QUICKEST WAY BACK.

BUT IT'S RIGHT OVER THE MEMORY DUMP. IF WE FALL WE'LL BE FORGOTTEN FOREVER!

WE HAVE TO DO THIS. FOR RILEY. JUST FOLLOW MY FOOTSTEPS.

HOHH... OKAY.

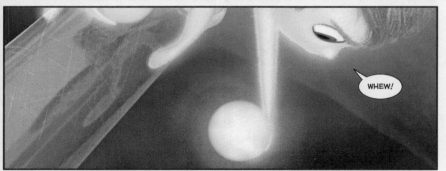

INSIDE OUT FUN BOOK

KNOCK KNOCK

HEY.

SO, UH... THINGS GOT A LITTLE OUT OF HAND DOWNSTAIRS.

YOU WANT TO TALK ABOUT IT?

COME ON. WHERE'S MY HAPPY GIRL?

OO OO OOO!

INSIDE OUT FUN BOOK

OHHH. HE'S TRYING TO START UP GOOFBALL.

COME ON. OO OOO OOO OOO!

CREEEEEEAKK!

AHHH! GO BACK! RUN! RUN! RUN!

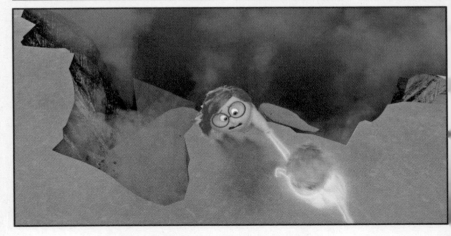

EEEERRRRRKKKK

THOOM!

BA-DOOOM!

INSIDE OUT FUN BOOK

165

INSIDE OUT FUN BOOK

INSIDE OUT FUN BOOK 167

I GET IT, YOU NEED SOME ALONE TIME. WE'LL TALK LATER.

OHH, JOY, WHERE ARE YOU?

WE HAVE A MAJOR PROBLEM.

Read on for another scene!

INSIDE OUT FUN BOOK

INSIDE OUT FUN BOOK

INSIDE OUT FUN BOOK

INSIDE OUT FUN BOOK

INSIDE OUT FUN BOOK

INSIDE OUT FUN BOOK

INSIDE OUT FUN BOOK

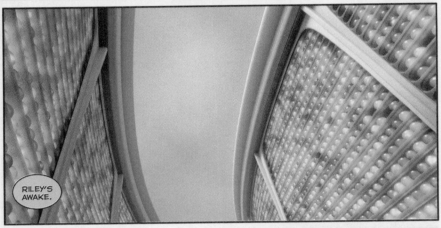

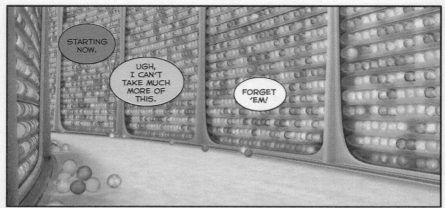

INSIDE OUT FUN BOOK

INSIDE OUT FUN BOOK

INSIDE OUT FUN BOOK

INSIDE OUT FUN BOOK

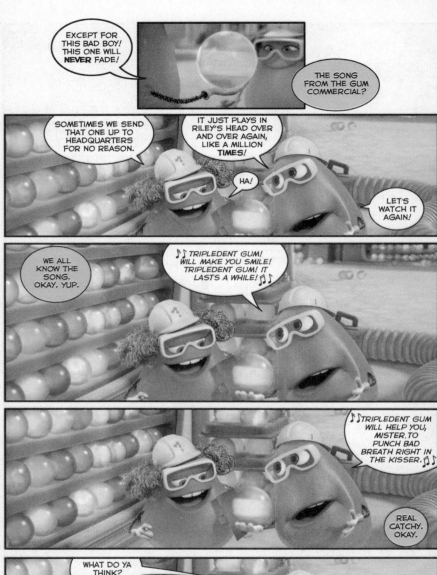

INSIDE OUT FUN BOOK

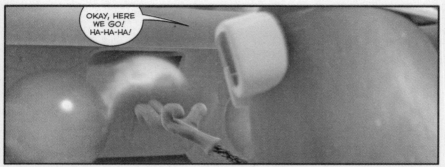

INSIDE OUT FUN BOOK

INSIDE OUT FUN BOOK

INSIDE OUT FUN BOOK

INSIDE OUT FUN BOOK

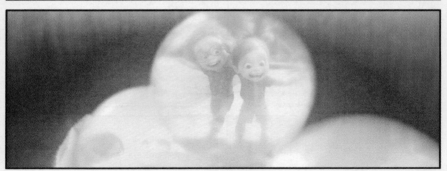

INSIDE OUT FUN BOOK

OHH, NOT FRIENDSHIP.

OH, RILEY LOVED THAT ONE. AND NOW IT'S GONE.

GOOD-BYE, FRIENDSHIP. HELLO, LONELINESS.

WE'LL JUST HAVE TO GO THE LONG WAY.

YEAH. THE LONG...LONG... LONG...LONG WAY. I'M READY.

INSIDE OUT FUN BOOK

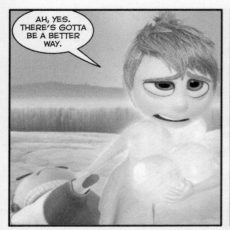

INSIDE OUT FUN BOOK

189

INSIDE OUT FUN BOOK

INSIDE OUT FUN BOOK

Read on for another scene!

INSIDE OUT FUN BOOK

INSIDE OUT FUN BOOK

INSIDE OUT FUN BOOK

INSIDE OUT FUN BOOK

INSIDE OUT FUN BOOK

INSIDE OUT FUN BOOK

INSIDE OUT FUN BOOK

JUST BECAUSE JOY AND SADNESS ARE GONE, I HAVE TO DO STUPID DREAM DUTY.

OKAY, HOW ARE WE GONNA WAKE HER UP?

WELL, SHE WAKES UP SOMETIMES WHEN SHE HAS A SCARY DREAM.

WE COULD SCARE HER.

SCARE HER? NO, SHE'S BEEN THROUGH ENOUGH ALREADY.

INSIDE OUT FUN BOOK

INSIDE OUT FUN BOOK

INSIDE OUT FUN BOOK

INSIDE OUT FUN BOOK

INSIDE OUT FUN BOOK

INSIDE OUT FUN BOOK

INSIDE OUT FUN BOOK

INSIDE OUT FUN BOOK

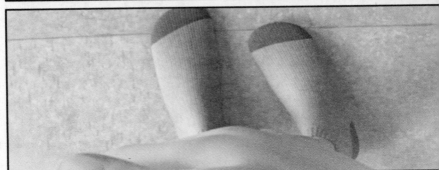

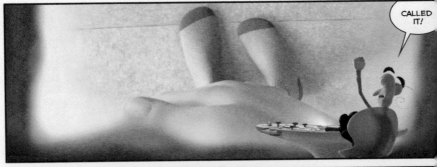

INSIDE OUT FUN BOOK

INSIDE OUT FUN BOOK

INSIDE OUT FUN BOOK

PSST. YOU'RE ON. GO!

INSIDE OUT FUN BOOK

INSIDE OUT FUN BOOK

INSIDE OUT FUN BOOK

HUH? SADNESS, WHAT ARE YOU DOING? COME BACK HERE!

INSIDE OUT FUN BOOK

IT'S JUST A DREAM, IT'S JUST A DREAM, IT'S JUST A DREAM...

UHHHHHHH.

INSIDE OUT FUN BOOK

game solutions

84
first
memory

85
half
empty glass

F

88
anger game

C - 5

86
different
emotions

87
emotional
crosswords

M
E
MEMORIES
JOY D
R I
SADNESS S
N G
G U
FEAR S
T

87
scrambled
console

5 10 8 7 1 9 4 3 6 2

89
abstract
thoughts
1-L, 2-G, 3-B,
4-H, 5-D, 6-F, 7-J,
8-K, 9-C, 10-I,
11-A, 12-E

92
sweet
sadness

C - 27

90
mind
maze

ABSTRACT THOUGHT

Disney · PIXAR

FINDING NEMO

JOE BOOKS
DISNEY·PIXAR
COMICS TREASURY
PREVIEW

INSIDE OUT FUN BOOK

INSIDE OUT FUN BOOK

INSIDE OUT FUN BOOK

INSIDE OUT FUN BOOK

MANY YEARS AGO, WHEN HE WAS JUST AN ELEMENTARY STUDENT...

...MIKE WAZOWSKI VISITED MONSTERS, INC. ON A FIELD TRIP.

I LEARNED EVERYTHING I KNOW FROM MY SCHOOL, MONSTERS UNIVERSITY. IT'S THE BEST SCARING SCHOOL THERE IS!

!

AS THE SCARE ACTIVITY STARTED ON THE SCARE FLOOR, THE KIDS WATCHED IN AWE...

WHOA! LOOK!

HEY! HOW ABOUT WE DO THE TALLEST IN THE BACK?

INSIDE OUT FUN BOOK

INSIDE OUT FUN BOOK

YEARS LATER, MIKE IS OFFICIALLY A STUDENT OF MONSTERS UNIVERSITY...

...DETERMINED TO ENTER THE SCARING SCHOOL AND FULFILL HIS DREAM.

MONSTERS UNIVERSITY ALSO HAS LOTS OF SUPER-COOL CLUBS AND EXTRACURRICULARS...

THEY'RE CRAZY DANGEROUS, SO ANYTHING COULD HAPPEN. YOU CAN TOTALLY DIE.

...AND IT'S WORTH IT! YOU GET A CHANCE TO PROVE YOU'RE THE BEST!

COOL.

SCARE GAMES

FINAL SIGN UP JAN 25

PROVE YOU'RE THE BEST

INSIDE OUT FUN BOOK

229

THAT NIGHT...

WHAT THE--?

ARCHIE? COME HERE BOY...

HEY! WHY ARE YOU IN MY ROOM?

SHHH!

WHERE'D HE GO?!

OVER THERE!

ARCHIE IS FEAR TECH'S MASCOT... I STOLE IT. GONNA TAKE IT TO THE RORS.

THE WHAT?

INSIDE OUT FUN BOOK

ROAR OMEGA ROAR? THE TOP FRATERNITY ON CAMPUS? THEY ONLY ACCEPT THE "HIGHLY ELITE"

WINDS OF CHA

WHAT AM I DOING? JAMES P. SULLIVAN IS THE NAME.

MIKE WAZOWSKI.

OK, ON THREE, I'LL LIFT THE BED, YOU GRAB THE PIG. READY?

ONE, TWO, THREE!

AHHH!

MY PIG!

MY HAT!

CATCH IT, SOMEBODY...

AH!

YEAH! RIDE IT TO FRAT ROW!

INSIDE OUT FUN BOOK

INSIDE OUT FUN BOOK

INSIDE OUT FUN BOOK

THE DAY OF THE SCARE FINAL...

I'M GONNA WIPE THE FLOOR WITH THAT LITTLE KNOW-IT-ALL TODAY.

YES, YOU ARE, BIG BLUE.

HEY, WAIT, WHAT ARE YOU DOING?

IT'S JUST A PRECAUTION. RORS CAN'T HAVE A MEMBER GETTING SHOWN UP BY A BEACH BALL...

TODAY'S FINAL WILL TEST YOUR ABILITY TO ASSESS A CHILD'S FEAR AND PERFORM THE APPROPRIATE SCARE...

DEAN HARDSCRABBLE IS HERE TO SEE WHO WILL BE MOVING ON IN THE SCARING PROGRAM AND WHO WILL NOT.

INSIDE OUT FUN BOOK

THE COMPLETE
BOOK AVAILABLE
IN STORES NOW.